Rapunzel Finds a Friend

By Ella Patrick

Illustrated by Jeffrey Thomas

A Random House PICTUREBACK® Book

Random House 🏠 New York

Copyright © 2017 Disney Enterprises, Inc. All rights reserved. Published in the United States by
Random House Children's Books, a division of Penguin Random House LLC, 1745 Broadway,
New York, NY 10019, and in Canada by Penguin Random House Canada Limited, Toronto,
in conjunction with Disney Enterprises, Inc. Pictureback, Random House, and the Random House
colophon are registered trademarks of Penguin Random House LLC.
randomhousekids.com
ISBN 978-0-7364-3747-9
Printed in the United States of America
10 9 8 7 6 5 4 3 2 1

Before Rapunzel knew she was a princess,
and before she left her tower as a young woman
and traveled to the kingdom, she was a little girl.
And she was very lonely.

Mother Gothel often left her alone for days. During that time, the only creatures Rapunzel saw were butterflies, bees, and sometimes a bird or two.

But the butterflies always flittered away.

The bees never got close enough to hug.

And no matter how many
seeds Rapunzel gave them, the
birds never stayed very long.

To fill her days, Rapunzel decided
to take up some hobbies.

First, she tried painting . . .

. . . but her finished artwork didn't look as good as she hoped it would.

Next, she tried baking . . .

. . . but her cake came out burned and black.

Finally, she tried gardening . . .

. . . but her seeds didn't sprout.

"This stinks," said Rapunzel.

"I can't paint, I can't bake, and
I can't grow even one strawberry."

Just as she was about to put away her shovel . . .

. . . Rapunzel noticed footprints in the dirt.

"Where did those come from?" she said.

She saw the same footprints
in her paint . . .

. . . and in her baking flour!

"This is a mystery," said Rapunzel. "I love mysteries!"

From then on, whenever Rapunzel worked on her art, she spilled a little paint.

When she baked, she scattered a little flour.

And when she gardened, she sprinkled
a little dirt. She wanted to see if the prints
would appear . . .

. . . and they always did!

Rapunzel still didn't know who was leaving
the footprints, so she kept painting, baking,
and gardening. That's how she became so
good at doing what she loved!

One day, Rapunzel was picking strawberries when she noticed one odd-shaped berry. She reached for it . . .

. . . and it changed color!

A small green chameleon stood
on the windowsill, frozen with fear.

"You must be the one who's been leaving the footprints!" said Rapunzel. The chameleon gave her a tiny nod. The lonely little girl hoped he would stay.

"My name is Rapunzel," she said. "I'll call you Pascal."

Pascal still looked shy. Rapunzel had an idea.
"Would you like some cake?" she asked, holding
out a big piece of strawberry shortcake.

As time went by, Rapunzel learned that Pascal
never said no to cake. And Pascal learned that Rapunzel
was the best friend a chameleon could ever ask for.

Ariel and Flounder swam home just in time to sing
a song of their own with Sebastian and his band.

. . . with a splash!

Just then, Ariel and Flounder heard
the most beautiful song. The whales were
saying goodbye . . .

"Flounder, I'm sorry I hurt your feelings," said
Ariel, hugging her friend. "It's okay to be afraid."

It was a mama whale and her baby!

"Now, *that's* a big baby!" exclaimed Flounder.

. . . the sea exploded
in a burst of bubbles!

Flounder's feelings were hurt. He swam away.
Ariel started to follow him, but suddenly . . .

"... enormous!"

"Oh, don't be such a big baby!" teased Ariel.

"Whales?" cried Flounder.

"But they're so . . ."

Ariel scanned the horizon but still saw nothing.
"Where are the whales?" she wondered out loud.

She swam to the surface with Flounder trailing behind her.

When they reached the edge of the reef,
Ariel looked out into the ocean. There were
no whales in sight.

"Wait for me, Ariel!" called Flounder
as he passed a school of jellyfish.

Ariel loved to sing, but she didn't want to miss the whales.

"I'm sorry, Sebastian, but we have an important appointment," said Ariel. She motioned to Flounder, and the two swam away.

A few minutes later, Ariel and Flounder came upon Sebastian. He and his band were setting up for a performance.

"You're just in time for a deep-sea duet!" he told them.